For Lynn and Holly

THIS IS A BORZOI BOOK PUBLISHED BY ALFRED A. KNOPF

Copyright © 2002 by Jarrett J. Krosoczka

www.randomhouse.com/kids

Library of Congress Cataloging-in-Publication Data
Krosoczka, Jarrett.
Baghead / by Jarrett J. Krosoczka. — 1st ed.
p.   cm.
Summary: Josh hides the bad haircut he gave himself by wearing a bag on his head, until his sister has a better idea.
ISBN 0-375-81566-X (trade) — ISBN 0-375-91566-4 (lib. bdg.)
[1. Hair—Fiction. 2. Haircutting—Fiction. 3. Humorous stories.] I. Title.

PZ7.K935 Bag   2002
[E]—dc21   2001038138

Printed in the United States of America
September 2002

10 9 8 7 6 5 4 3 2 1

First Edition

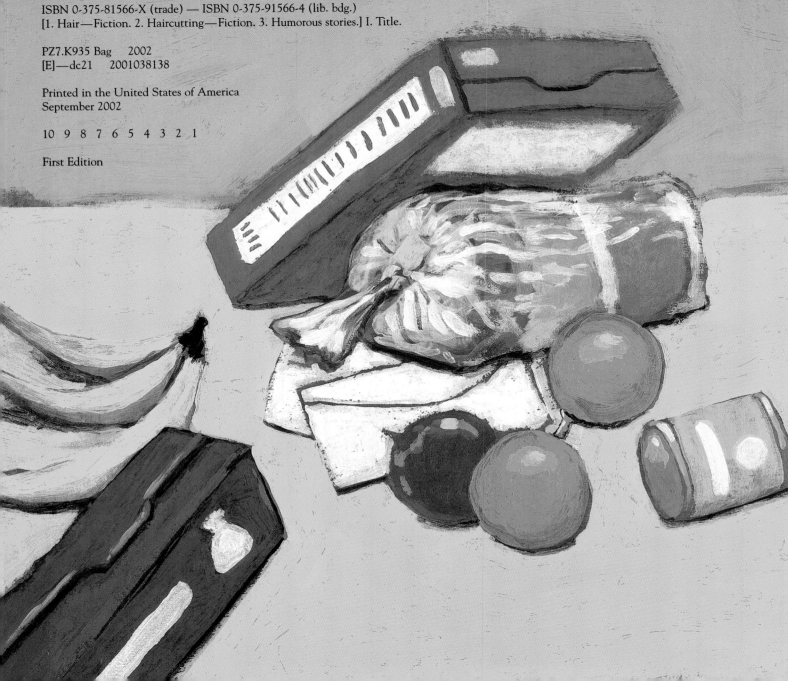

Baghead

Jarrett J. Krosoczka

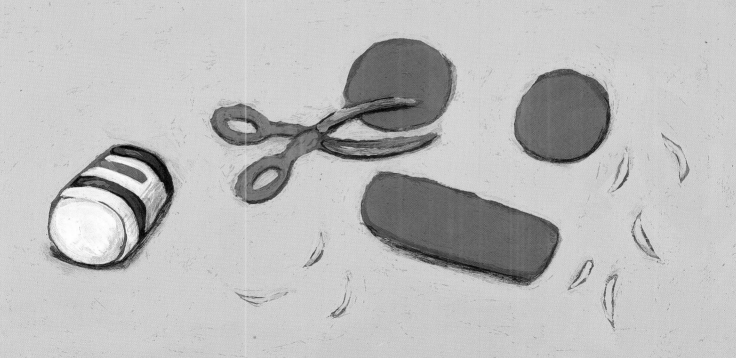

Alfred A. Knopf, New york

On
Wednesday
morning,
Josh had
an idea.

A very **BIG** idea.

A very **BROWN** idea.

A very **BIG,**
BROWN,
BAG idea.

Josh thought it was a good idea.

His mother did not.

"You can't eat breakfast with a paper **bag** on your head!"

she said.

But Josh did.

He piled a forkful of scrambled eggs into his mouth and didn't leave a crumb on his plate.

His bus driver, Mrs. Boyle,
opened the door
and stared at him.

"You crazy kid!
You can't go to
school like
that!"
she exclaimed.

But Josh climbed on the bus
and rode to school.

His teacher, Mr. Tucker,
wasn't amused.

"Don't tell me
you **forgot** your
book report,"

he said.

JOSH didn't. He stood in front of the class and told them about a boy who met a giant slug.

His soccer coach, MS. O'Neil,
frowned.

"How do you
plan to play
like **that?**"

she demanded.

His dad picked him up
after the game.

"was it
crazy-hat
day
at school?"

he asked.

"Nope," said Josh.

At dinner, his mother didn't say anything. Neither did his brother or his dad.

"Why are you wearing a bag, JOSH?" his little sister asked.

"Because I tried to cut my own hair," said Josh.

On Thursday morning, Josh's sister had an **idea.**

A very **COOL** idea.

A very SPIKY idea.

A very COOL, SPIKY, MEGA-HOLD GEL idea.